Sports Files

SAMMY SOSA

Rick Burke

Heinemann Library
Chicago, Illinois

Designed by Wilkinson Design
Printed in Hong Kong/China by Wing King Tong

05 04 03 02 01
10 9 8 7 6 5 4 3 2 1

Library of Congress Cataloging-in-Publication Data

Burke, Rick, 1957-
   Sammy Sosa / Rick Burke.
      p. cm. — (Sports files)
Includes bibliographical references (p.) and index.
   ISBN 1-58810-113-4
   1.   Sosa, Sammy, 1968—-Juvenile literature. 2. Baseball players—Dominican
Republic—Biography—Juvenile literature. [1. Sosa, Sammy, 1968- 2. Baseball players.]
I. Title. II. Series.
   GV865.S59 B87 2001
      796.357'092—dc21
[B]   00-011875

Acknowledgments
The author and publishers are grateful to the following for permission to reproduce copyright material: Michael S. Green/AP Photo, p. 4; Reuters Newmedia Inc./Corbis, p. 5; Victor Baldizon, p. 6; John Riley/AP Photo, p. 7; Corbis, p. 8; Victor Baldizon, p. 9; Victor Baldizon, p. 10; Victor Baldizon, p. 11; Jonathan Daniel/Allsport, p. 12; Victor Baldizon, p. 13; Victor Baldizon, p. 14; Doug Pensinger/Allsport, p. 15; Brad Newton, p. 16; PhotoDisc, p. 17; Texas Rangers, p. 18; Janice E. Rettaliata/Allsport, p. 19; Mike Fisher/AP Photo, p. 20; Al Behrman/AP Photo, p. 21; AP Photo, p. 22; John Gaps III/AP Photo, p. 23; Rob Tringali Jr./SportsChrome, p. 24; Beth A. Keiser/AP Photo, p. 25; Jose Luis Magana/AP Photo, p. 26; Victor Baldizon, p. 27; Stephen J. Carrera/AP Photo, p. 28; Keith Bedford/AP Photo, p. 29.
Cover photograph by Rob Tringali Jr./SportsChrome.
Special thanks to John Klein and Victor Baldizon.

Every effort has been made to contact copyright holders of any material reproduced in this book. Any omissions will be rectified in subsequent printings if notice is given to the publisher.

This is an unauthorized biography. This subject has not sponsored or endorsed this book.

Some words are shown in bold, **like this.** You can find out what they mean by looking in the glossary.

Contents

Sammy, Sammy, Sammy

On September 18, 1999, Sammy Sosa made history. Sammy had just hit his 60th **home run** of the **season.** He would always be remembered as one of the greatest home run hitters of all time. He became the first player in baseball history to hit more than 60 home runs in two different seasons.

Sammy Sosa wants to play baseball the best that he can. He works hard and practices a lot.

Sammy is so popular that kids in Japan look up to him, too.

Sammy Sosa is more than just a good baseball player. He has become a **role model** for thousands of kids around the world. Sammy has made a lot of money playing baseball. He uses some of that money to help other people.

Family

Sammy Sosa was born on November 12, 1968, in the **Dominican Republic.** He has three brothers named Luis, Jose, and Juan. He also has two sisters named Raquel and Sonia.

Sammy, far right, never lets his **success** in baseball keep him from spending time with his family.

Sammy and his wife (far left) celebrated his 32nd birthday with his mother in the Dominican Republic.

Sammy's name at birth was Samuel Montero. His father, Bautista, died when Sammy was seven years old. Sammy's last name became Sosa when his mother, Lucrecia, married another man.

The Dominican Republic

The **Dominican Republic** is a country in the Caribbean Sea. It is south of the United States. The country is on the same island as another country called Haiti.

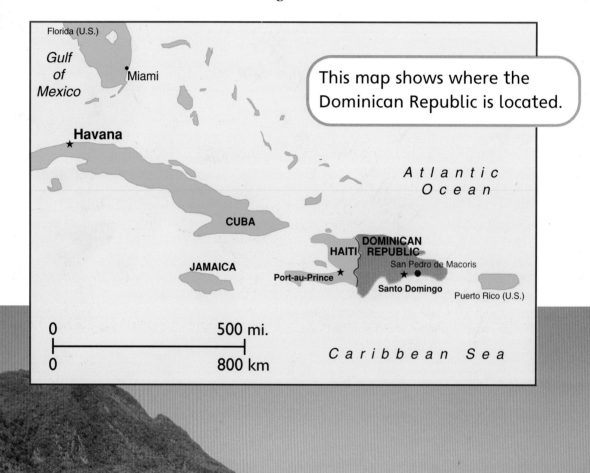

This map shows where the Dominican Republic is located.

This street in San Pedro de Macoris says, "Sosa, your people love you."

Sammy grew up in the city of San Pedro de Macoris. The city has an important **port**. Ships sail in and out of the **harbor** with **goods** from all over the world. Sammy lived in a very poor part of the city called *Barrio Mexico.*

Childhood

Sammy's family was poor. Sammy had to stop going to school when he was very young. He had to go to work to make money so his family could buy food.

People in Sammy's hometown stop in shops to watch him play.

This shoeshine boy is doing the same job that Sammy had when he was young.

When Sammy was nine, he became a **shoeshine boy** in the *Parque Central* area of the city. Many other boys worked there too. Sammy's bright smile helped him get lots of customers. On good days, he made as much as two dollars to bring home to his mother.

Pelota!—Baseball

Playing baseball was a way for many Dominican boys to earn money. If they played well enough, they could go to the United States to play in the **major leagues.** Major league baseball players make a lot of money!

In the **Dominican Republic** and other Spanish speaking countries, *pelota* means ball.

Here, Sammy is with Juan Marichal, a **Hall of Fame** pitcher from his home town.

Other boys from San Pedro de Macoris had made it to the major leagues. Juan Marichal, George Bell, Tony Fernandez, and Joaquin Andujar had become rich playing baseball. They were heroes to many people in the Dominican Republic.

First Team

Sammy played on his first baseball team when he was fourteen years old. He was so good that the other teams wanted him to play with the older kids instead. Sammy's team did not have uniforms. The boys were so poor they did not even have caps to wear.

These mitts and balls are similar to what Sammy used when he was young.

Kids often have to make their own bats and balls.

Sammy did not have enough money to buy a baseball glove. He made his own out of empty paper milk cartons. He cut off the bottom, stuck his hand inside, and tore holes for his fingers. Sammy played catch using a rolled up sock for a ball.

Away from Home

When Sammy was sixteen, a **professional** baseball team in the United States, the Texas Rangers, wanted him to play for their team. They would give Sammy $3,500 to play on their team. Sammy agreed to the **contract.** He gave the money to his family to help them buy food and clothes.

While with the Texas Rangers, Sammy practiced hard and played in the outfield during games .

Being in a big city in Texas, far away from his family, was hard for Sammy.

Sammy had to get used to the way people lived in his new country. He also had to learn a new language, English. Sammy could not even go to restaurants, because he did not know how to say what he wanted. He called or wrote to his mother almost every day.

Early Career

Sammy was afraid that he would not stay in the **major leagues.** He worked very hard and practiced as much as he could. He wanted to keep his job. "This is my job. I only know how to play baseball," said Sammy.

Sammy warms up before batting in a Texas Rangers game.

While with the Chicago White Sox, people started seeing that Sammy could become a great baseball player.

Sammy was **traded** twice early in his **career.** In 1989, he left Texas to play for the Chicago White Sox in Illinois. He was there for two and a half years. Then the White Sox traded Sammy to the Chicago Cubs.

Practice and a Promise

Sammy's way of thinking helped him become successful. He said, "I just want to play every day, do my best, and go home happy." He was often the first player to get to the ballpark. He would also stay for extra batting practice and lift weights to become stronger.

Sammy's skills kept getting better while he was playing for the Chicago Cubs.

Sammy shows his control as he slides into third base.

No matter where Sammy played, he always thought of home. Sammy believes that a big reason he made it to the **major leagues** was because he wanted to help his family. "Everywhere I go, they are with me," Sammy once said. "That's why I play good now, because I have something I promised and I want to keep my promise."

The Race Is On!

The **major league** record for the most **home runs** hit in one **season** was 61. The record had been set by Roger Maris in 1961. Mark McGwire of the St. Louis Cardinals started the 1998 season quickly. He had hit 24 home runs by May 24.

Roger Maris held the record for the most home runs in one season for 37 years!

Sammy thought Mark McGwire would win the 1998 home run race.

Sammy had hit just nine home runs during the same period. Then he hit twenty in the month of June. The race to beat the home run record was on!

A Magic Season

Sammy and Mark battled for the rest of the **season**. Each of them wanted to break the **home run** record. Mark was the winner. He hit 70 home runs, while Sammy finished with 66.

Sammy was not the first to break the home run record. But he was only the second player to hit more than 61 home runs in one season.

Sammy is shown here after being named the Most Valuable Player in his league.

Sammy was happy to be named the **Most Valuable Player** in the National **League** at the end of the 1998 season. He was even happier to help his team, the Chicago Cubs, get to the **playoffs** for the first time in nine years.

A Hurricane at Home

At the end of the 1998 baseball **season,** Hurricane Georges hit the **Dominican Republic.** Many people were without food or a place to live. Sammy and other Dominicans living in the United States wanted to help. They gathered supplies and sent them to the island.

Here, supplies are being unloaded in Santo Domingo to help the victims of Hurricane Georges.

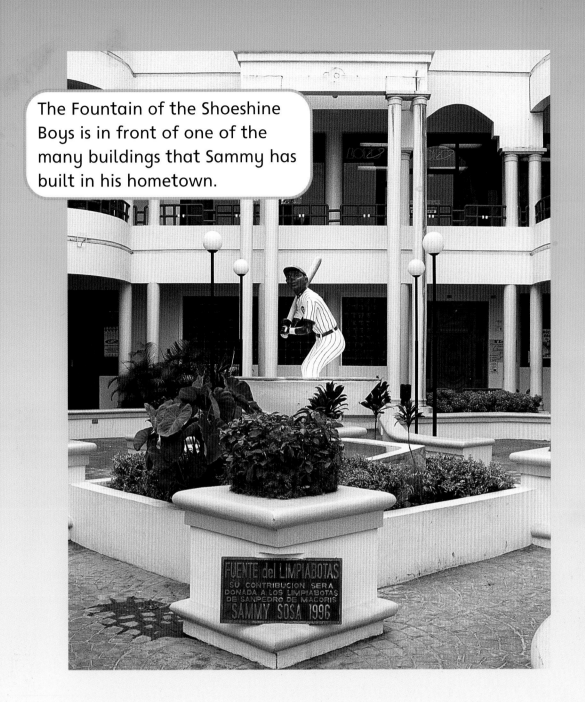

The Fountain of the Shoeshine Boys is in front of one of the many buildings that Sammy has built in his hometown.

Sammy is a hero to many people in the Dominican Republic. He has never forgotten his home. There is a statue of Sammy in the Fountain of the **Shoeshine Boys** in San Pedro de Macoris. All the coins tossed into the fountain are given to local shoeshine boys.

Family and the Future

After every **home run** he hits, Sammy makes the same sign to the crowd. He thumps his heart with his fingers in a "V" shape and blows two kisses. One kiss is for his mother. The other is for his family, friends, and fans. Sammy has his own family now. His wife's name is Sonia. They have four children—Keysha, Kenia, Sammy Junior, and Michael.

Sammy makes his sign after hitting his 51st home run of the 1999 **season**.

The Sammy Sosa Foundation paid for the **surgery** that saved Yelisa Espinal's life.

Sammy will always help people, even after his baseball **career** is over. Through the Sammy Sosa **Foundation,** he helps children in the United States and the **Dominican Republic.** He has bought computers for schools, ambulances for hospitals, and thousands of gifts for children.

Star File

SAMMY SOSA

1983	Played on his first baseball team when he was fourteen
1985	Signed his first professional contract with the Texas Rangers when he was sixteen
1989	Played in his first major league game against the New York Yankees and collected two hits
	Traded to the Chicago White Sox
1992	Traded to the Chicago Cubs
1993	First player in Cubs' history to hit more than 30 home runs and steal more than 30 bases in a single season
1995	Selected to play in his first All-Star game
1998	Hit 66 home runs
	Named the National League's Most Valuable Player
	Won the Roberto Clemente Award for outstanding service to the community
1999	Became the first player to hit 60 or more home runs two seasons in a row

Glossary

career   job that a person does for most of his or her life

contract   agreement between two people

Dominican Republic   country in the Caribbean Sea, south of the United States

foundation   group that helps people in need

goods   products that are bought and sold

Hall of Fame   museum honoring people who have gained fame in a particular field, such as sports

harbor   part of a sea or lake that is a safe place for ships to stop

home run   hit that allows the player to run to all four bases

league   group of teams

major leagues   top two groups of professional baseball teams, the National League and the American League

Most Valuable Player   award given to the player who has done the most to help a team during a season; often considered to be the player who had the best year

playoffs   set of games between the best teams at the end of a sports season

port   place where ships load and unload goods

professional   type of team that pays its players

role model   person that someone looks up to

season   period of time during which a sport is played

shoeshine boy   boy who polishes people's shoes to make money

success   gaining of fame from other people

surgery   to fix or repair injured parts of the body

traded   given to a different team for another player

More Books to Read

Driscoll, Laura. *Sammy Sosa: Home Run Hero.* New York: Putnam Publishing Group, 1999.

Kirkpatrick, Rob. *Sammy Sosa: Home-Run Hitter.* New York: Rosen Publishing Group, Inc., 2000.

Muskat, Carrie. *Sammy Sosa.* Bear, Del.: Mitchell Lane Publishers, Inc., 1999.

Index